Suzann

Diar

for

Nichola

Suzanne's Diary for Nicholas

James Patterson

Thorndike Press • Chivers Press
Waterville, Maine USA Bath, England

This Large Print edition is published by Thorndike Press, USA and by Chivers Press, England.

Published in 2001 in the U.S. by arrangement with Little, Brown and Company, Inc.

Published in 2001 in the U.K. by arrangement with Headline Book Publishing Ltd.

U.S. Hardcover 0-7862-3297-8 (Basic Series Edition)
U.S. Softcover 0-7862-3298-6
U.K. Hardcover 0-7540-1707-9 (Windsor Large Print)
U.K. Softcover 0-7540-9106-6 (Paragon Large Print)

The text of this Large Print edition is unabridged.
Other aspects of the book may vary from the original edition.

Set in 16 pt. Plantin by Christina S. Huff.

Printed in the United States on permanent paper.

British Library Cataloguing-in-Publication Data available

Library of Congress Cataloging-in-Publication Data

Patterson, James, 1947–
    Suzanne's diary for Nicholas : a novel / James Patterson.
        p.   cm.
    ISBN 0-7862-3297-8 (lg. print : hc : alk. paper)
    ISBN 0-7862-3298-6 (lg. print : sc : alk. paper)
    1. Mothers and sons — Fiction.   2. Loss (Psychology) — Fiction.   3. Infants — Fiction.   4. Large type books.
    I. Title.
PS3566.A822 S8 2001b
    813'.54—dc21   2001027094

For those who have loved, and lost,
and loved again

For Robin Schwarz, whose valuable assistance
and big heart are much appreciated

Also, thanks for the help —
Mary, Fern, Barbara, Irene, Maria, Darcy,
Mary Ellen, and Carole Anne

Most of all, for Suzie and Jack; and for Jane

Katie

Katie Wilkinson sat in warm bathwater in the weird but wonderful old-fashioned porcelain tub in her New York apartment. The apartment exuded "old" and "worn" in ways that practitioners of shabby chic couldn't begin to imagine. Katie's Persian cat, Guinevere, looking like a favorite gray wool sweater, was perched on the sink. Her black Labrador, Merlin, sat in the doorway leading to the bedroom. They watched Katie as if they were afraid for her.

She lowered her head when she finished reading the diary and set the leatherbound book on the wooden stool beside the tub. Her body shivered.

Then she started to sob, and Katie saw that her hands were shaking. She was losing it, and she didn't lose it often. She was a strong person, and always had been. Katie whispered words she'd once heard in her father's church in Asheboro, North Carolina. "Oh, Lord, oh, Lord, are you *anywhere*, my Lord?"

She could never have imagined that this small volume would have such a disturbing effect on her. Of course, it wasn't just the diary that had forced her into this state of confusion and duress.

No, it wasn't just Suzanne's diary for Nicholas.

She visualized Suzanne in her mind. Katie *saw* her at her quaint cottage on Beach Road on Martha's Vineyard.

Then little Nicholas. Twelve months old, with the most brilliant blue eyes.

And finally, Matt.

Nicholas's daddy.

Suzanne's husband.

And Katie's former lover.

What did she think of Matt now? Could she ever forgive him? She wasn't sure. But at least she finally understood some of what had happened. The diary had told her bits and pieces of what she needed to know, as well as deep, painful secrets that maybe she didn't need to know.

Katie slipped down farther into the water, and found herself thinking back to the day she had received the diary — July 19.

Remembering the day started her crying again.

On the morning of the nineteenth, Katie had felt drawn to the Hudson River, and then to the Circle Line, the boat ride around Manhattan Island that she and Matt had first taken as a total goof but had enjoyed so much that they kept coming back.

She boarded the first boat of the day. She was feeling sad, but also angry. Oh, God, she didn't know what she was feeling.

The early boat wasn't too crowded with tourists. She took a seat near the rail of the upper deck and watched New York from the unique vantage point of the brooding waterways surrounding it.

A few people noticed her sitting there alone — especially the men.

Katie usually stood out in a crowd. She was tall — almost six feet, with warm, friendly blue eyes. She had always thought of herself as gawky and felt that people were staring at her for all the wrong reasons. Her friends begged to differ; they said she was close to breathtaking, stunning in her strength. Katie always responded, "Uh-huh, sure, don't I wish." She didn't see herself that way and knew she never would. She was an ordinary, regular person. A North Carolina farm girl at heart.

She often wore her brunette hair in a long braid, and had since she was eight years old. It used to look tomboyish, but now it was supposed to be big-city cool. She guessed she'd finally caught up with the times. The only makeup she ever wore was a little mascara and sometimes lipstick. Today she wore neither. She definitely didn't look breathtaking.

Sitting there on the top deck, she remembered a favorite line from the movie *The African Queen*: "Head up, chin out, hair blowing in the wind, the living picture of the hero-eyne," Bogart had teased Hepburn. It cheered her a bit — a *titch*, as her mother liked to say back home in Asheboro.

She had been crying for hours, and her eyes were puffy. The night before, the man she loved had suddenly and inexplicably ended their relationship. She'd been completely sucker punched. She hadn't seen it coming. It almost didn't seem possible that Matt had left her.

Damn him! How could he? Had he been lying to me all this time — months and months?

Of course he had! The bastard. The total creep.

She wanted to think about Matt, about what had happened to separate them, but she wound up thinking of times they'd shared, mostly good times.

Begrudgingly, she had to admit that she had always been able to talk to him freely and easily about anything. She could talk to Matt the way she talked to her women friends. Even her girlfriends, who could be catty and generally had terrible luck with men, liked Matt. *So what happened between us?* That's what she desperately wanted to know.

He *was* thoughtful — at least he *had been.* Her birthday was in June, and he had sent her a single rose every day of what he called "your birthday month." He always seemed to notice whether he'd seen her in a certain blouse or sweater before, her shoes, her moods — the good, the bad, and occasionally the stressed-out ugly.

He liked a lot of the same things Katie did, or so he said. *Ally McBeal, The Practice, Memoirs of a Geisha, The Girl with the Pearl Earring.* Dinner, *then* drinks at the bar at One if by Land, Two if by Sea. Waterloo in the West Village; Coup in the East; Bubby's on Hudson Street. Foreign movies at the Lincoln Plaza Cinema. Vintage black-and-white photos, oil paintings that they found at flea markets. Trips to NoLita (North of Little Italy) and Williamsburg (the new SoHo).

He went to church with her on Sundays, where she taught a Bible class of pre-schoolers. They both treasured Sunday afternoons at her apartment — with Katie reading the *Times* from cover to cover, and Matt revising his poems, which he spread out on her bed and on the bedroom floor and even on the butcher-block kitchen table.

Tracy Chapman or Macy Gray, maybe Sarah Vaughan, would be playing softly in the background. Delicious. Perfect in every way.

He made her feel at peace with herself, completed her circle, did *something* that was good and right. No one else had ever made her feel that way before. Completely, blissfully at peace.

What could beat being in love with Matt?

Nothing that Katie knew of.

One night they had stopped at a little juke bar on Avenue A. They danced, and Matt sang "All Shook Up" in her ear, doing a funny but improbably good Elvis impersonation. Then Matt did an even better Al Green, which completely blew her away.

She had wanted to be with him all the time. *Corny, but true.*